W9-BXD-137

YES, DEAR

Text copyright © 1992 by Diana Wynne Jones
Illustrations copyright © 1992 by Graham Philpot
The Author asserts the moral right to be
identified as the author of this work.

First published in Great Britain in 1992 by HarperCollins.
First published in the United States in 1992 by Greenwillow Books.
All rights reserved. No part of this book may be reproduced
or utilized in any form or by any means, electronic or mechanical,
including photocopying, recording, or by any information storage
and retrieval system, without permission in writing from the
Publisher, Greenwillow Books, a division of William Morrow
& Company, Inc., 1350 Avenue of the Americas, New York, NY 10019.

Printed and bound in Great Britain   First American Edition
10 9 8 7 6 5 4 3 2 1

Library of Congress Cataloging-in-Publication Data
Jones, Diana Wynne.
Yes, dear / Diana Wynne Jones ; pictures by Graham Philpot.
          p.   cm.
"First published in Great Britain in 1992 by HarperCollins"—T.p. verso.
Summary: Kay catches a magic golden leaf that creates all
kinds of wondrous things, but everyone is too busy to listen
to her tell about it.
ISBN 0-688-11195-5
[1. Magic—Fiction.]   I. Philpot, Graham, ill.   II. Title.
PZ7.J684Ye   1992   [E]—dc20   91-17733   CIP   AC

YES, DEAR

Diana Wynne Jones

Illustrated by Graham Philpot

GREENWILLOW BOOKS, NEW YORK

MERIDEN PUBLIC LIBRARY
Meriden, Conn.

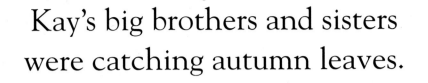

Kay's big brothers and sisters
were catching autumn leaves.

2450486
jE

Kay tried to catch one too,
and tried, and tried, and caught one.
It was bright and yellow and shiny.

"Look!" Kay shouted.
"I've caught a magic golden leaf!"
"Yes, dear," Kay's brothers and sisters said kindly.
"Run along and play and don't bother us now."

"I *know* it's a magic leaf,"
Kay said.
"I shall wish that my sand pies
and my sand cakes
and my sand pancakes were real."

And they were.
Then Kay made sand pizzas
and sand ice creams and sand sandwiches,
and they were real too.
"I shall tell Mum," said Kay.

Kay found Mum in a flowerbed.
"Mum, Mum!" Kay shouted.
"Look at my magic golden leaf.
It made my sand pies real!"

"Yes, dear," Mum said kindly.
"Run along and play
and don't bother me now.
I'm trying to do the garden."

 "But it is a magic leaf!" said Kay. "I shall wish for a big flower of my own." Kay's flower was a huge rose so big that Kay could walk inside it. It smelled wonderful. There was a caterpillar round a corner, and it looped up when it saw Kay.

"I'm going to be a moth one day," the caterpillar said. "What are you going to be?"

"Very big," said Kay. "I shall tell Dad."

Kay found Dad in the kitchen
making a lot of bubbles in the sink.
"Dad, Dad!" Kay shouted.
"Look at my magic golden leaf!
It made a big rose
with a caterpillar inside
and real sand pies."
"Yes, dear," Dad said kindly.
"Run away and play and
don't bother me now.
The washing machine has
broken, and I'm trying to
wash my socks."

"**B**ut it is a magic leaf!" said Kay. "I shall wish for bubbles now."

Kay's bubbles came in crowds. Some were like rainbows, some were like jewels, some had castles in, and dragons, and ships, and towers, and faces.

When Kay
poked them,
they went
Blop!
and burst.
"I must tell someone,"
said Kay.

MERIDEN PUBLIC LIBRARY
Meriden, Conn.

Kay's sisters were in the bedroom by then, playing dress up with the bedspreads. "Look at my magic leaf!" Kay shouted. "It made big colored bubbles and a rose with a caterpillar inside and real sand pies." "Yes, dear," Kay's sisters said kindly. "Run away and play and don't bother us now. We are being kings and queens."

"ut it is a magic leaf!" said Kay.
"I shall wish to be dressed up too."
Kay's clothes were ten times finer
than any bedspread.
They were silk and satin with
knobby jewels and feathery lace
and rattling gold net, and Kay wore
a spiked crown and pointed shoes
with cold buckles.
The patchwork quilt turned
into Kay's kingdom and
stretched way into
the blue distance.

"I shall show my brothers," said Kay.

Kay's brothers were twanging guitars
and thumping drums.
"Look, look!" Kay shouted.
"My magic leaf has made me fine clothes now
and colored bubbles
and real sand pies."
"Yes, dear," Kay's brothers
said quite kindly.
"Run away and play and
don't bother us now.
We are busy
with our music."

"But it is a magic leaf!" said Kay. "I wish for music too."
Kay's music came from
mermaids and
marching soldiers
and strange woodland creatures
and pipers piping

and fiddlers three,
but Kay's brothers
did not hear it.
"Nobody will listen to me,"
said Kay.
"There must be *somebody*
I can tell about
my magic leaf."

Kay found Granny
sitting shelling peas.
Before Kay could speak,

Granny looked up
and said,
"I see you've caught a magic leaf."

"Oh yes," said Kay.
"It made music and fine clothes
and big bubbles

and a rose with a caterpillar inside
and real sand pies,
but nobody will listen when I tell them.
How did *you* know?"

"Because I caught one once,"
said Granny.
"It did wonderful things,
but everyone was too busy to
listen when I told them."
"Just like me," said Kay.
"Yes, dear," said Granny.
"Just like you."

Meriden Public Library
Meriden, CT 06450

A2090 245048 6

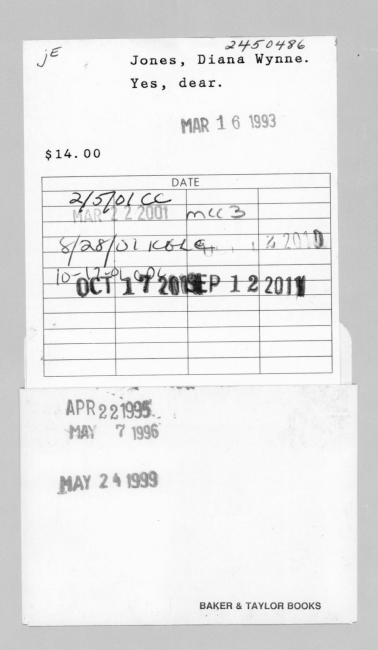

jE

2450486

Jones, Diana Wynne.

Yes, dear.

MAR 1 6 1993

$14.00

DATE		
2/5/01 CC		
MAR 2 2 2001	mcc3	
8/28/01 KOLQ		L 3 2010
10-17-06 COK	OCT 17 2013 SEP 1 2 2011	

APR 2 2 1995
MAY 7 1996

MAY 2 4 1999

BAKER & TAYLOR BOOKS